JE

P9-CFZ-237

3 5674 02578291 4

DETROIT PUBLIC LIBRARY

CHASE BRANCH LIBRARY
17731 W. Seven Mile Rd.
Detroit, MI 48235
935-5346

DATE DUE

AUG 2 0 1996	APR 1 9 2000
MAR 2 0 1997	MAY 1 0 2000
MAR 2 0 1997	
OCT 1 3 1997	
OCT 2 2 1997	
NOV 1 8 1997	
JAN 2 6 1998	
MAY 2 7 1998	
APR 0 1999	
APR 0 1999	
APR 0 1 1999	

BC-3

CH

JUN 5 '98

POPPA'S NEW PANTS

For my in-laws, Charles and Leslie Medearis,
and in memory of Ethel and F.D. "Poppa" Taylor, with love
—A.M.

To Mom and Dad
—J.W.

Text copyright © 1995 by Angela Shelf Medearis
Illustrations copyright © 1995 by John Ward
ALL RIGHTS RESERVED
Printed in the United States of America
FIRST EDITION

Library of Congress Cataloging-in-Publication Data
Medearis, Angela Shelf, 1956–
Poppa's new pants / Angela Shelf Medearis ; illustrated by John
Ward.—1st ed.
p.   cm.
Summary: Poppa finds a pair of lovely pants, only six inches too
long, but Grandma Tiny, Big Mama, and Aunt Viney are all too tired
to hem them before church.
ISBN 0-8234-1155-9
[1. Trousers—Fiction.]   I. Ward, John (John Clarence), ill.
II. Title.
PZ7.M51274Po   1995   94-20489   CIP   AC
[E]—dc20

POPPA'S NEW PANTS

Angela Shelf Medearis

illustrated by John Ward

Holiday House/New York

The house was in an uproar. Grandma Tiny had been tearing around all morning like a Texas tornado. Big Mama and Aunt Viney were coming for a visit. Grandma Tiny wanted everything and everyone to look nice when her mother and sister arrived. Poppa and I had beaten so many rugs, washed so many windows, and moved around so much furniture that we'd sweated a bucketful.

We were both glad when Grandma Tiny told us to hitch up old Buck and go to the store.

"Howdy, Poppa. Howdy, George," said Mr. Owens, the storekeeper, when we arrived. "What can I do for y'all today?"

"I've got a list of things to get for Tiny," said Poppa. "Her mama and sister are coming up from Kansas City. She's about to bust a gusset making sure everything's just right."

Mr. Owens laughed as Poppa handed him the list. Poppa and I wandered around the store while Mr. Owens filled our order. We were having a good time looking at the shiny new farm equipment when Poppa spied a pile of pants stacked on a table. Most of them were plain black or brown corduroy.

"Mighty poor pickings here," Poppa said. But when he reached the bottom of the pile, he let out a long whistle.

"George," he said, holding up a pair for me to see. "What do you think about these?"

They were gray pants with a red gambler's plaid pattern. The fabric was as velvety soft as old Buck's nose.

"They look real nice, Poppa," I said, "but they must have been made for a giant! They're way too long for you."

Poppa held the pants against his waist. The extra fabric was so long, it draped onto the floor.

"Well," said Poppa, "so they are. But I bet your grandma Tiny could hem them before church in the morning."

Poppa winked at me and added the long-legged pants to the pile of things we were buying for Grandma Tiny. I winked back and picked out the fattest peppermint stick I could find. Poppa took out his worn leather wallet and paid for everything.

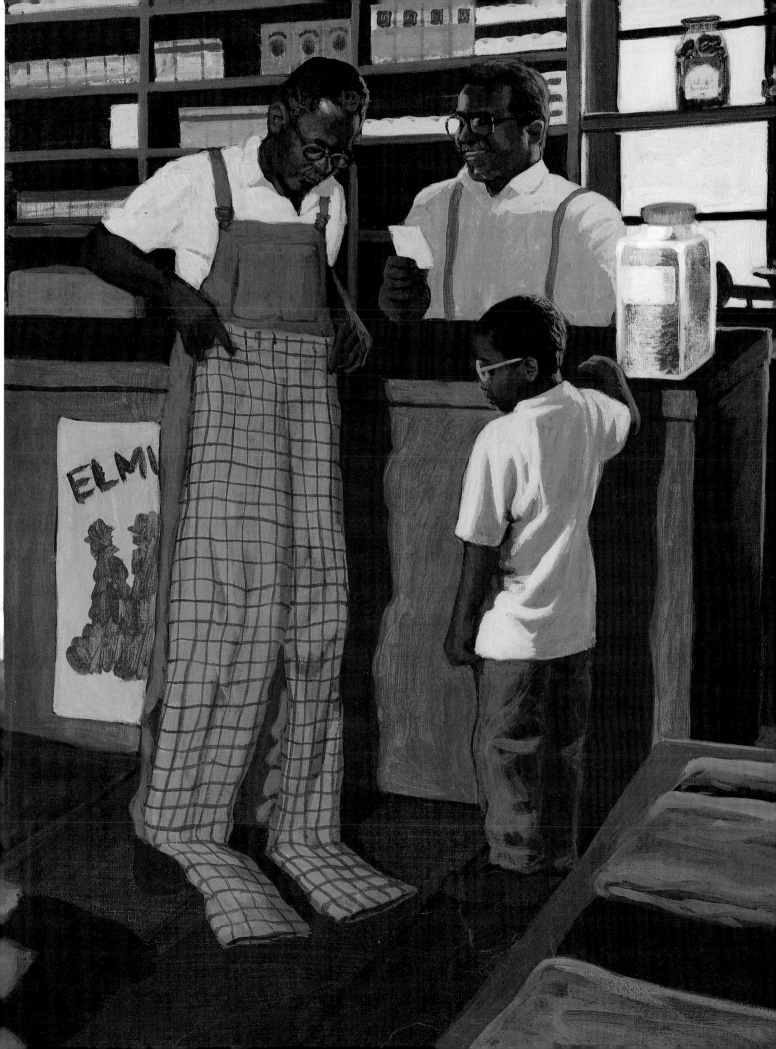

Big Mama and Aunt Viney had arrived by the time we got home. They must have been mighty glad to see me because they snatched me from the wagon like I was a rag doll. Big Mama hugged me so hard that she squeezed the breath right out of my body. Then Aunt Viney and Big Mama took turns covering my face with red lipstick. I almost drowned in a sea of sloppy wet kisses.

"Come on in, y'all," Grandma Tiny finally said. "Supper's just about ready."

Grandma hustled Poppa inside so she could get the groceries put away. I ran after them as fast as I could.

Poppa set down a bag of groceries and unwrapped his new pants. He proudly stretched them across the table for Grandma Tiny, Big Mama, and Aunt Viney to see.

"Nice fabric," said Big Mama.

"What a beautiful pattern," said Aunt Viney.

"Yes, they're mighty pretty pants," said Grandma Tiny. "But they're way yonder too big for a tee-ninchy little man like you, Poppa. Looky here! They're almost long enough to use as a tablecloth."

"Well, honey," said Poppa, "I was hoping you could cut off about six inches and hem them tonight so I could wear them to church tomorrow."

"Oh, honey," said Grandma Tiny, "I'm plum worn out! I've been cooking and cleaning since sunrise. As soon as supper's finished and Mama and Viney get settled in, I'm going to bed!"

"Okay," said Poppa. He turned to Aunt Viney. "Do you think you could hem my pants for me, Viney?"

   "Oh Brother-in-law, dear," Aunt Viney said, "I'd love to, really I would, but my eyes are troubling me from driving so long. I need to get some sleep."

   "I understand," Poppa said. He looked hopefully at Big Mama and held up his new pants.

   "Sorry, son," Big Mama said. "I've got arthritis in my knee joints so bad I can hardly move. I'm looking forward to just resting this evening."

   "That's all right, y'all," Poppa said sadly. He put his new pants across the rocker to be mended. Then he went out on the back porch to wash up for supper.

Grandma Tiny called everyone to dinner. She'd cooked everything from chicken and dressing to chocolate cake. The table looked like it was going to buckle in the middle. Supper was delicious, but we were all so tired, conversation was mighty poor. As soon as Poppa was finished eating, he said good night all around and got ready for bed.

Grandma Tiny, Big Mama, and Aunt Viney usually have a good long gossip spell when they get together. But this time, the three women quietly finished their chores and turned in for the night. Big Mama and Aunt Viney had taken over my room. Grandma Tiny made a pallet for me on the kitchen floor while I changed into my pajamas. I took my glasses off and put them on the kitchen table.

I kicked the covers around until I found a soft spot to snuggle into. I could hear Poppa snoring gently and the dark house moaning softly as everyone settled down for the night.

I wasn't used to sleeping in the kitchen. It was kind of spooky. The huge wooden china cabinet and big, black woodburning stove crouched in the corners. The grandfather clock wheezed awake every hour and rang out the time. After awhile, the moon crept into the room making a big pool of bright, white light by the rocking chair. I jumped when a tree limb scraped against the window screen. I was just drifting off to sleep, when I spotted something out of the corner of my eye.

A small, white shape was moving slowly into the kitchen. I was so scared that at first, I forgot to breathe. I squeezed my eyes closed and pulled the covers over my head.

I told myself over and over that there were no such things as ghosts. But I didn't believe it. I could hear whatever it was slowly coming closer . . . and closer . . . and closer. It must have brushed up against the rocking chair because the chair creaked softly back and forth, back and forth. I held my breath until I thought I'd burst. I heard a snip, snip, snip and a funny rustling. Then all was quiet.

It was too quiet! After an hour that seemed like days, I pulled the covers off my head. I finally made my eyes open so I could peek over the edge of the quilt. The ghost-thing was gone! I was tempted to go sleep on the floor by Poppa and Grandma Tiny.

I lay quietly for awhile, mustering up my courage. Just when I thought it was safe to make a run for it, I spied a tall, thin, ghostly white figure drifting into the room. I threw the covers back over my head. My heart was thumping like old Buck's after a long, hard run. I heard the rocking chair creak back and forth, back and forth. Then I heard that funny snip, snip, snip, rustle, rustle sound. After awhile, all was quiet again.

I gave up on the idea of going into Poppa and Grandma Tiny's room. I kept the covers over my head and prayed for morning to come. I must have dozed off because when I opened my eyes, I couldn't figure out where I was. It was so hot, I started to throw the quilt off my head, but then I remembered about the ghosts.

I pulled the covers down inch by inch. I pried open my eyes and slowly looked around the room. A big, white ghost was drifting through the doorway, and it was coming toward me!

I dove down to the foot of the pallet and curled up into a ball. I was shaking all over like a wet dog. I felt something brush past me heavily. Then the rocking chair moaned loudly as it creaked back and forth, back and forth. I heard that snip, snip, snip, rustle, rustle sound and all was quiet again. My teeth were rattling so loud, I thought some of them were going to fall out! I stayed balled up under those blankets like an armadillo for the rest of the night.

"George! George!" The sound of Grandma Tiny's voice woke me the next morning as she whipped the covers off my head.

"Boy, why in the world are you sleeping under all those blankets as hot as it is?" Before I could answer she said, "Go get washed up. We need to hurry if we're going to make it to church on time."

Bright yellow sunlight filled the room. It was morning and I was still alive. I checked to make sure all my limbs were in place. Everything was where it should be. I put on my glasses and stumbled sleepily through the door. Poppa was already on the back porch shaving. I didn't want to say anything about last night. Three ghosts in one evening! I'd never heard a story like that! Besides, maybe I was dreaming. The rocking chair and everything else in the room looked just like they always did. I mumbled good morning to Poppa and splashed cold water on my face. I'd just finished brushing my teeth when Grandma Tiny came out on the porch. "Poppa," she said, "hurry up and come inside. There's a surprise for you!" As Poppa went into the kitchen, I followed behind, wondering what all the fuss was about.

Grandma Tiny, Big Mama, and Aunt Viney were gathered around the table. I said good morning and quickly sat down. I didn't want to give Big Mama and Aunt Viney a chance to hug and kiss the life out of me again. Besides, I had had a hard time getting that red lipstick off my face. Grandma Tiny was smiling fit to beat the band. She had Poppa's new pants folded across her arm.

"Honey," said Grandma Tiny, "I got to thinking about what a wonderful husband you are and about how much you wanted to wear these pants. So I got up last night, cut off six inches, and hemmed them for you."

Poppa's smile lit up the room.

"Oh no," said Aunt Viney. "I got to thinking about what a sweet brother-in-law he is, so I got up last night, cut off six inches, and hemmed them up, too!" Poppa stopped smiling and looked at Aunt Viney.

"Well sir, would you listen to this," said Big Mama. "I couldn't rest for thinking about what a good son-in-law he is. So I got up last night, cut six inches off those pants, and hemmed them up, too!"

My mouth dropped open. So these were the ghosts that were haunting me last night!

Poppa grabbed his new pants from Grandma Tiny and held them up to his waist. The beautiful, soft gray pants with the red gambler's plaid gently unfolded to his knees.

We all stared at what was left of Poppa's new pants. Poppa hung his head and clutched the pants to his chest. His thin shoulders started to shake. Then all of a sudden, Poppa burst out laughing.

"Well, these pants aren't too long now!" he said.

He put them on and smiled at us. Then he danced around the room in the cut-off pants. He looked so funny we couldn't help laughing. After a long while he wheezed to a stop. Grandma Tiny hugged Poppa around the waist.

"Honey," said Grandma Tiny gently, "don't you worry about those old pants. Next time we go to the store, I'll help you pick out some pants that fit." Poppa hugged her back.

"Come on, y'all," said Big Mama, looking at the clock. "We'll miss Sunday School but we can still make it to church." We scurried around getting ready.

We pulled up in front of Rock Hill Church just in time for the eleven o'clock service. Grandma Tiny, Aunt Viney, and Big Mama looked real pretty in their Sunday going-to-meeting hats. They rustled through the wooden doors of the sanctuary like walking flower gardens. Poppa looked nice too, although he was wearing the same black pants he wears every Sunday. And I must say, I looked mighty sharp in my brand new gray knickers with the red gambler's plaid.

The "ghosts" had hemmed them too short for Poppa, but they were just right for me.